The Mysterious Amish Suicide

Hannah Schrock

Table Of Contents

Leah had to remind herself to breathe. A pressure filled her chest, as though something sat on it. She could hardly think, move, do anything without a great deal of willpower. It was an effort to stay upright. She wanted to lie on her bed and cry her eyes out.

Sometimes she felt dizzy, her head spinning. It made her think of the games she'd play with Levi when they were small. They would see how far they could walk in a straight line after spinning around in circles, giggling together as they stumbled around and fell.

She was still dizzy, only she was without Levi. She had never been without him. He'd been her one constant since she was born. He was gone.

The police officers shifted in place before her, which gave her a view of the wall behind them, and the clock there. Was it that late already? No wonder she felt dizzy and weak—she hadn't eaten in hours.

Rain beat on the roof, pouring down in front of the windows in a torrent. It had been raining hard since not long after Jonah reached her at the farmer's market to tell her the news about Levi. As though the heavens opened up to cry the tears she worked so hard to contain.

It didn't seem real, and not just because it had only been a handful of hours since Jonah gave her the news of her brother's disappearance. It would never seem real, no matter how much time passed. Her brother, jumping into the river.

She glanced over at Amos, who sat by the hearth with two other police officers. It was a rare sight, so many Englischer officers in her little kitchen. Her community stayed away from them as a rule, choosing to solve their problems on their own. The Amish were a self-contained people. This was far too big a problem to keep to themselves, however, and Leah preferred the police become involved if it meant finding her brother's body and finding out what really happened to him. She would never believe he jumped of his own free will.

Amos said he did, however. She listened to what he told the officers, the same story he'd been telling for hours. "We were on an errand for my father, inquiring about a new shipment of wood. I noticed Levi seemed melancholy, though he wouldn't share his feelings with me. I noted how unusual it was for him to behave that way, since he didn't normally. Whenever I spoke to him, I had to repeat myself to be heard. He wasn't paying attention—he was too troubled, too distracted. We stopped to talk with a few of my father's customers who asked about work they waited on. Levi slipped away when I didn't notice."

One of the officers cleared his throat. "What made you think to look for him by the river?"

"I passed the river along my route," he explained. "I finished walking to the mill, then turned back. I saw him on the bridge not far from the mill, along the river. Nobody ever goes there—it's in disrepair and half-concealed by high grass. I called out to him, but it was as if he didn't hear me. At first, I thought he was only looking into the water, thinking. He looked just as sad as he had before. I began to walk toward him, but he jumped into the water before I could reach him."

Leah closed her eyes, squeezing them shut against the mental image of her brother leaping into the river. What could have inspired him to do something like that? It made no sense. It went against everything she knew to be true about her brother, who she'd always thought she knew better than anybody in the world —better even than her best friend, Jonah.

Jonah stood in a corner of the room, away from the conversation. He was always there, though, always the single calming presence she relied on. Just as he'd been for her entire life—so steady, strong, reliable. She needed him more than ever.

His eyes met hers, and she saw the sadness and sympathy in them. There was nothing he could say to make her feel better, but just his presence gave her a little extra strength.

She wished he could do the same for her father, who looked completely broken. Almost no one could get through to him. His only son—first his wife, then his son.

"We'll have to wait for the rain to stop, I'm afraid." Leah looked up at the lead officer, who continued to explain himself. "The river is so swollen, our teams can't find much of anything. It shouldn't rain for but another hour or two, according to the forecast."

Only another hour or two. Considering that it felt like a lifetime since Jonah found her, begging her to go home to be with her father after hearing about Levi's jump, it would be another lifetime before the searchers could continue their work.

Leah stood, going to Jonah with eyes full of tears. "How could this be?" she whispered.

"I don't know," he murmured. "We'll never know, I guess."

She looked at him, seeing the pain in her heart reflected in his eyes. He was never as close with Levi as he was with her, but he appeared just as shaken as she felt. It was too unbelievable to be true, and yet there was no denying it. Amos was certain he saw Levi jump, and there was little chance he could have survived the fall. It was clear nobody there had any hope of her brother coming home alive.

An officer walked downstairs, his feet heavy on the wooden boards. In his hand, he held a sheet of folded paper. He'd gone through Levi's room—it was difficult for Leah to sit idly by and allow it to happen, as she felt it was an invasion of her brother's privacy. In her heart, he was still alive. He would walk through the door any minute, soaked to the skin, with a story of slipping from the bridge and being swept downstream. He'd always been a strong swimmer, and he had a way of making even the dreariest experience sound interesting in the telling.

The officer handed the paper to another man, then another. They all skimmed the lines of neat, handwritten script. Leah resisted the urge to tell them to mind their own business. Another invasion.

Jonah must have read the tension in her, for he placed a calming hand on her arm. "Anything that will help them," he murmured. "They must do their job." Leah let out a sigh of defeat. He was right—he usually was, almost always more level-headed than she was. While Leah was quick to action, Jonah sat back to consider all possible outcomes before committing himself one way or another.

Eventually, the paper found its way into Leah's hands. By the light of the oil lamp over the sink, she and Jonah read its contents. A letter from Rachel. Leah gasped softly. "Rachel Troyer?" she murmured.

"Not Troyer for much longer," Jonah observed quietly. "She says she'll be married to another man from her community next month."

Tears filled Leah's eyes. Oh, poor Levi.

She turned to the officers. "Did you find the envelope to this letter?"

One of the nodded, holding it out to her. The postmark bore all the evidence she needed. It was dated the day before, meaning it had to have arrived that morning. It was all too much to make sense of.

"Who was this Rachel Troyer to your brother, Miss Kauffman?" The man had kind eyes and a gentle voice. He wasn't one of the gruff, all-business officers around her. He seemed to genuinely sympathize with her confusion and grief. Just the same, Leah didn't want to go into Levi's past with Rachel for fear of what it implicated.

Jonah's hand once again reassured her, squeezing her arm gently. Yes. It was for the best. She cleared her throat prior to speaking.

"Levi met Rachel at a party three summers ago. She was visiting from Ohio at the time, staying with cousins. Levi…fell in love with her." Leah blushed furiously as her father's sad, empty eyes met hers. She hated talking about Levi's personal life with strangers, or even in front of her father. It hadn't been a secret, Levi's feelings for Rachel, but it felt as though she betrayed him nonetheless.

"Did they have a relationship?" one of the officers asked.

"They wrote all the time, sometimes twice a week, maybe more— whenever Levi could get a little time away. Rachel came back every summer, too. That was as far as their relationship went. Our lives are not like yours."

The kind officer smiled. "We know that. You don't need to explain.

Do you know of any of the other letters around here?"

Leah shook her head in all honesty. "I don't know that he kept them, or where."

He nodded. "From the sound of the letter, Rachel was letting him down. Breaking it off."

Leah glanced at the paper in her hand. "Yes, it looks that way. She's to marry another man, at her father's orders." Brief, shining anger flashed through her. Rachel's father had been the only thing standing between them all along. Were it not for him, Leah knew Rachel would happily have moved to Lancaster to marry Levi.

"So a three-year relationship, ended very suddenly by letter today. A jump from a secluded section of the river." The policemen looked at one another. Leah heard the resigned certainty in their voices. Her shoulders slumped. They thought they had the case solved already, she knew.

"I'm sorry to say this," the kind officer said. He took a step closer to Leah. "We have no reason to believe your brother didn't commit suicide."

Leah clenched her fists, raising her chin in defiance.

"I disagree," she said, her voice ringing strong and clear. All eyes shifted to her.

"Leah, please." Jonah sounded deeply concerned. "Don't do this to yourself." As always, his very presence calmed her—but nothing would make her change her mind.

"Miss, I know it seems unbelievable…"

Leah cut the officer's words off with a flash of her eyes on his. He stood down, a sheepish look on his face. "It seems more than unbelievable, sir. It seems unthinkable. Life is the greatest gift Gott gives us. I know my brother—no matter his grief, he would not throw away a precious gift."

Everyone shifted uncomfortably. "I understand," the kind officer said, looking around at the other police to quiet them. "Please understand, Miss Kauffman, that we need to look at all possibilities when doing our work. We can't rule anything out."

She nodded, staying silent. It was no use arguing—they didn't know Levi. They weren't Amish. They were so used to seeing crime and death, they probably didn't hold human life in the same value people such as she and Jonah did. They were immune to the beauty and wonder of it. There would be no convincing them. They would always see her as a grief-stricken sister who refused to accept the truth. She expected them to pat her on the head and send her on her way.

***

Hours later, the kitchen was quiet and virtually empty once again. Only Jonah remained, sitting at the table with a cup of coffee. Leah sat across from him, and she knew he was waiting for her to speak. She also knew he would give her all the time she needed.

Amos had left long before the police did. He was helpful, concerned, clearly distraught. "I should have stopped him. I should have known." There was no way for him to know, and she told him so—besides, she thought, there was no guarantee Amos hadn't missed something concealed in the tall, thick grass all around the bridge. Such as another person, or someone in the water. It would be just like Levi to jump in to help someone else with no thought for his own safety.

Not long after Amos left, her father went to bed. She'd gone so far as to help him up the stairs, as he didn't look as though he could manage it on his own. He was foggy, lost. It reminded Leah of the terrible early days right after her mother's death. Eight years had passed, and Leah still remembered clearly the pain of those days. In the years since, she'd believed that was the hardest time of her life. The past several hours had served to change her opinion.

"Are you hungry?" she asked Jonah.

"I could eat, though it's nothing you should worry about right now. I can fix something."

She smiled. "Doubtful."

"Are you hungry?" he asked.

"No, but I know I need to eat." She knew all too well, and it was with a rueful smile that she stood to put food together. When she was twelve, she'd had no experience with grief. It had been easy to fall into a habit of refusing food, not sleeping well, putting all her energy into caring for her father and older brother. She'd worked herself into exhaustion, to the point where their doctor had ordered her to bed for three days.

She put out a loaf of bread, cheese, cold meat and leftover pie from the refrigerator—one of the few conveniences their ordered allowed. Despite his hesitation, Jonah dug into the food with vigor. Leah smiled softly as she watched him eat.

She rubbed her eyes, feeling more tired than she could remember feeling since those ugly days after a sudden brain hemorrhage ended her mother's life. She felt all cried out, like there wasn't a tear left in her body…though she knew there would be more time to cry before all was said and done. Levi was still out there somewhere, his body floating along the water or maybe caught up in some reeds along the riverbank. She nearly choked on a mouthful of food at the thought.

She pushed the ugly thought from her mind, reminding herself how strong she needed to be for her father. His health was never strong to begin with, though he did the best he could with the help of assistants at the bakery…and Levi.

"Thank you for being here with me," Leah murmured, staring down at the plate of food she had no desire to eat. She forced herself to take a bite of her sandwich, then another.

"Of course," Jonah replied. His blue eyes were so kind, as always, his voice full of gentleness. She wondered if he was ever anything but gentle, patient, kind.

"You may think it's nothing, but it means a lot to me," she insisted. "I don't know what I would do alone."

"You never have to be alone."

Even in her state of grief, Leah blushed. Jonah had a way of saying things which hinted at a deeper meaning. He didn't always speak that way, but when he did Leah invariably felt a flutter in her stomach.

She sighed. "I can't believe he's gone. There's something inside me which won't let me believe it."

He nodded thoughtfully, and took a long time before speaking. That was his way, always thinking things through. "It's quite a shock. More than that, it seems out of character for him."

"Exactly. He wasn't a depressive person. He didn't go around with a frown on his face. He wasn't always happy—who is? But he wasn't the type to act rashly. He wouldn't have thrown his life away like this."

Jonah shrugged. "Who's to say, though? The letter from Rachel… none of us can say what goes on in a person's heart. None of us knows how we would react in a situation such as that. When we love a person, and know they can never be ours. Not only that, but he knew she would be another man's wife." He shook his head. "I'm not sure how I would feel if that happened to me."

Another flutter in her stomach. Even in the deepest grief, Jonah had a way of reaching her heart.

"He could have talked to me about it. He should have. Why didn't he? We could always talk about things."

"I'm sure he wasn't thinking clearly."

Leah shook her head. "No. I refuse to believe this."

"Leah…"

"I mean it, Jonah. He wasn't a rash person. I knew him—I know him," she corrected. She couldn't wrap her mind around the notion of referring to him in past tense. "I know my brother like I know myself. This isn't something he would do. Something else happened. I don't know what. Either there was somebody in the water who he tried to save, or somebody…pushed him." It sounded silly even to her ears, but she couldn't allow herself to entertain another theory."

Jonah sighed as though he knew better than to try to change her mind.

"I need to find out what really happened," she said, leaning across the table toward him. "I need to. I can't live not knowing."

He regarded her in his usual quiet manner, his eyes going over her face. She stared at him with great intensity, willing him to understand what she meant and felt. Of all people, she had to get him to understand.

And he did, as he always did. "I'll help you in any way I can."

She smiled, glowing from within. Just those few words were enough to give her extra strength.

"What would I do without you?" she asked.

"You'll never need to find out." He smiled, taking her plate and his to the sink, then putting the rest of the food away. She was too tired to argue, and yawned as though to punctuate the thought.

"You need some rest," he observed. "It will be a long few days coming up."

Leah nodded. "I know," she said. "I know all too well."

"I'll be here for whatever you need." He turned to her, leaning against the sink. "I mean it. Whatever you need. I hate to think of you going through this all alone."

She smiled wearily. "I'm not alone. I have Gott, not to mention my father."

"Yes, Gott is always there. I fear you'll be caring more for your father than anything else, though."

Leah nodded, chewing her lip. "I know. I hate to think of it that way, but I know."

"Remember," Jonah said, taking his hat from the hook by the door. "No one expects you to be strong all the time. It's important to take care of yourself, too." He saw himself out, and Leah waved as he left. Normally, she would have shown him to the door, but nothing was normal. She felt rooted to the spot, looking around the empty kitchen, wondering if she would ever feel truly happy again. Nothing would be the same without Levi—her first friend, and the best one she'd ever had aside from Jonah.

There was no use fighting the idea that he wasn't coming back. She knew he was gone, felt it in her heart. He would always be with her in spirit, but she would never hear his laugh again. He would never tease her or go out of his way to make her smile when she had a difficult day.

She took the stairs to the second floor one slow step at a time. It almost felt like too much to ask of herself, the simple act of climbing the stairs. Her body and soul were so tired, aching.

Gott would give her strength, and she said a string of prayers as she rested in bed after changing into her nightdress. There was nothing but silence in the house—her father was either sleeping or, more likely, saying his own prayers. Or grieving. Leah wished there was something she could say to lessen his pain, but knew there was nothing. He'd lost his only son.

After at least an hour with no sleep in sight, Leah got out of bed and tiptoed down the hall. She intended to go to Levi's room—somehow, she thought it might feel less painful there. She might be able to pretend he was still with her.

She was too late. Her father had already fallen asleep there. The door was open, he was fully dressed. As though he'd fallen onto the bed in a fit of grief and cried himself to sleep.

Leah tiptoed away without closing the door. She didn't want him to wake up to find that she'd observed him. What could she do for him? She could get to the bottom of how Levi had met his end, for one. Then came the question of how she would do that.

She knew that whatever methods she'd use, she'd have to do it on her own. It would only deepen her father's grief if he found out.

It wasn't until late the following morning that Levi's body was found, tangled in some reeds along the bank of the river. He'd floated more than five miles downstream, thanks to the force of the rushing, storm-swollen water. There were stones in his pockets, most likely placed there to weigh him down. He had a head wound, along with many injuries the police believed would be caused by a fall like that from the bridge.

When Jonah came to the kitchen door to break the news gently, Leah knew before he said a word what the news was. There was so much pain in his eyes—not only because he didn't want the unhappy task of telling her, but because he and Levi had always been friendly. The three of them had known each other ever since childhood. It was assumed in those days that the boys would be the ones to form a deep and lasting bond, but it was Leah, instead, who had attracted Jonah's attention. Some of the adults teased behind half-hidden smiles that there was more to Jonah's friendship than met the eye, but Leah had refused to pay them any mind.

Still, Levi was special to just about everybody in the community, so it was with a look of great sadness and a voice heavy with grief that Jonah told Leah her brother's body had been discovered and pulled from the water.

She wasn't worried for herself when she heard the news—she'd been expecting it. If anything, there was relief in knowing her brother could be laid to rest. She was concerned for her father, and immediately fled the house to dash the half-mile to the bakery.

She hadn't been able to believe it when he'd come downstairs early in the morning, as though it were any other day. He'd even asked why breakfast wasn't yet prepared.

"Daed," she'd whispered. "You're not considering going to the bakery this morning?"

"And what not? It is not the Sabbath," he'd pointed out.

"No, it isn't. But...I'm not sure you should go to work. I mean...I'll be all alone..." She'd searched her mind for reasons why he shouldn't go which didn't include her fear for him. If she made it sound as though she needed his help, his comfort, it might be more effective than telling him he couldn't emotionally or physically handle the demands of a busy day at the bakery—one which would inevitably be busier, thanks to the presence of the community gossips who would surely want to get a look at Mr. Kauffman in his hour of grief.

"I'm sure Jonah will keep you company," he'd said, distracted. He was shutting it all out, she'd realized. His way of coping with the grief. She would have preferred he stay home and join her in prayer, but when her mother had passed Leah had learned there was a different method of grieving for every person. Her grief wasn't the same as her father's, just as the way she dealt with it wouldn't be the same as his.

So she was alone when Jonah came with the news, and he stayed behind as she ran to the bakery to comfort her father. By the time she got there, the news had spread. She arrived breathless, flushed, strands of auburn hair escaping her kapp. All eyes turned to her, eyes full of pity. She acknowledged them but did not stop to speak. They were respectful enough to give her room to move through the bakery to the back room, which was where she found her father.

He sat alone in a chair, facing a window. She put a tentative hand on his shoulder, and he looked up at her as though he didn't recognize her at first. He was too far away, too lost.

"I thought it was all a mistake," he murmured, shaking his head. "I thought he would be found alive. I did."

Tears filled her green eyes. "I know, Daed. I had hoped for the same."

"He's not coming back now, is he?"

"No. He's not. We have to lean on each other, now. You have to let me take care of you. Please, Daed."

He nodded, patting her hand with the same distracted manner he'd taken earlier in the day. Leah resigned herself to the fact that it would take him a lot of time to get over the shock of losing his son. She helped him from the chair, then walked him out of the bakery. Mr. Stoltzfus, who had long been one of the family's closest friends, offered to drive them home. Leah accepted, and within minutes they were home again. Leah helped her father to bed—he was in shock, she knew, and he'd do best to sleep while she dealt with the aftermath.

Jonah was waiting for her in the kitchen. Leah wondered if he would always be there for her, or if he would eventually find another girl to spend his time with. What would she do when that day came? It was almost as unthinkable as losing Levi.

"You were good to stay," she murmured, putting on a pot of coffee.

"Is there anything I can do?" he asked.

"There will be many people here," she said, chewing her lip. "I don't know if I can handle them. I don't know if I can handle this." She realized she was shaking, and Jonah rushed across the room to meet her. He put a friendly arm around her shoulders, squeezing to bolster her.

"I know you can do this," he murmured. "I know you can. I'm here for whatever you need."

She smiled weakly up at her best friend, then turned her head at the sound of buggies coming toward the house. Neighbors, friends, all of them bearing food and prayers. They meant well, but Leah fretted at the thought of keeping a brave face for them. The arm around her shoulders reminded her she wasn't alone, not really.

Once again, she wondered what she'd ever do without him.

***

Two days later, it was time to lay Levi to rest.

The community was distraught over the loss of a vibrant young man, one who so clearly loved Gott and wished to do His bidding. Why would he turn his back on everything he'd ever been taught? It went against everything the Amish held most dear.

Over the two days between the discovery of his body and the funeral services, Leah had heard many times how unthinkable it was that Levi would kill himself. She agreed with them.

One person didn't agree, though. The one person who'd been with Levi that final day.

"He was so sad," Amos would say to anyone who would listen. "If I hadn't seen how troubled he was, I never would have believed it myself. I blame myself for this."

He was saying something similar the day of the funeral service, when Leah approached and happened to overhear. She turned to him with a frown, shaking her head.

"Amos, this isn't your fault. You couldn't have known what Levi would do."

He shook his head, curly blond hair framing his face beneath the crown of his hat. His deep brown eyes were pained, stormy. "No, I've known him long enough to know better. We worked together for years. He was like a brother to me—my daed always saw him that way. I should have kept him close by me at all times, when I saw how depressed he was."

Amos had been talking with Martha, one of Leah's friends, when Leah approached. She repeated Leah's assurance that Levi's actions weren't his fault, then turned to Leah once Amos walked away.

"How are you holding up?" she asked, placing an arm around Leah's waist. Her earnest face turned upward to meet the taller girl's gaze. Leah smiled affectionately down at her friend.

"As well as can be expected, I suppose," she admitted. "I feel like I might fall apart when this is all over. Like Gott is only allowing me to bear this much because I have to be in front of people. Once it's over and they go home and forget all about this, I'll have time to break down."

"Do you really think you'll break down?" Martha asked, grimacing.

"I don't know," Leah replied, chewing her lip. "I've been pushing it all down, inside me. Trying to help my daed, trying to help the police."

"Help the police?" Martha repeated. "What are they asking you to do? It seems to me they should leave you alone, now."

"They're not forcing me," Leah murmured, looking around to be sure she wasn't overheard. The mourners didn't seem to pay much attention to her, aside from looking at her with sad, tear-filled eyes. Otherwise, they were respectful enough to give her breathing room.

"So what is it you're doing with them? Or for them? I don't understand."

"They can't prove Levi killed himself," Leah whispered.

"Nobody can. I mean, nobody was there to know exactly what happened. Even Amos was too far away to know what went on."

"I know, I know. That's what's troubling me, though. There has to be some way to find out exactly what brought this all about." She knew how crazy it sounded—there was probably no such way. She knew, too, that it was possible she was wrong about Levi. He might have despaired just enough to throw away his life. Only he and Gott knew what really happened. She couldn't let go of the nagging feeling that something was dreadfully wrong, though.

"Oh, Leah." Martha hugged her. "I'm so sorry. I'll be praying for you and your father."

Jonah approached them, and Martha gave him a smile before disappearing into the crowd.

"How are you?" he asked.

"Tired, but all right." She looked around, seeing an identical expression of pain on the faces of everyone she saw. She noticed something for the first time, and turned to Jonah. "Have you seen Mr. Yoder here?"

He shook his head. "No, I thought it odd."

"He and Levi were so close," Leah murmured. It seemed strange for Amos to be there without his father. Mr. Yoder had employed Levi for years as an employee at his furniture shop.

"Sometimes I think he saw Levi as more of a son than he saw Amos," Jonah observed, keeping his voice low.

"What makes you say that?"

"The way I saw Mr. Yoder treat the two of them. If I hadn't known better, I would've thought Levi was his son, not Amos."

This was news to Leah. She'd known Amos's father was a sort of mentor to Levi, wishing to encourage his natural talent for woodworking and furniture making, but hadn't heard that it went any further than that.

"Everybody knows Mr. Yoder is hard on him," Lead replied. "That's the sort of man he is, though. I don't think it was anything personal. He's just as tough on all his employees. He was tough on Levi, too."

"Yes, but Levi rose to the challenge," Jonah pointed out. "Amos has never been very good at what he does. I'm sure Levi must have told you."

"No, not at all. You know how he is—was," she corrected, her heart sinking. "Never wanting to brag, always shining the light on others. I'm sure he tried to highlight Amos's work."

"Oh, he did. Only there wasn't much to highlight." Jonah shook his head. "It was an uncomfortable position for him."

"I can imagine," Leah mused. She'd never liked Amos very much. He always seemed furtive, as though there was more than met the eye. Probably because Mr. Yoder didn't like him. She'd never known anything but love in her family, so she couldn't imagine what it would feel like to be constantly berated for her shortcomings. Mr. Yoder didn't have much patience, so any shortcomings Amos had would be amplified by his father's critical eye.

The rest of the day was a blur for Leah, as she stood by her brother's grave. It all seemed like a terrible nightmare—more than once did she look around, wondering if anyone else realized how surreal it all was.

It was real. The raw chill in the air was real. The feeling of her father's arm through hers was real. From time to time, he would tremble. She did all she could to remain a strong, supportive presence…even as she yearned to stop being strong. It would be such a relief to lay down her strength and allow herself to experience the deep, aching pain in her heart.

There would be time for that.

She looked at the simple wooden box in which her brother's remains would rest. She knew he wasn't really in that box—his soul was elsewhere. That didn't make it any easier to know he was right there, so close, yet so far.

None of it made sense. Even the passage of two days did not help her understand any better. She'd done a lot of thinking back to the many conversations they'd had, the sort of easy conversations two people fall into when it's been a long day and they're both tired. How many evenings had they spent sitting together by the fire? Leah would work on mending or knitting. Levi would carve little bits of wood. They would laugh quietly together, sharing stories from the day.

"Why don't you go to Ohio?" she'd once asked him. He'd only just Gotten a letter from Rachel that day, and he'd been lamenting the fact that they were so far away from each other. It was months and months before she'd come back for a visit.

"What do you mean?" His green eyes, so like hers, and burned with fierce intensity.

"Well, if you care for her, why not go there to be with her? Rather than spending years living miles apart. You could make a good life there, in that community. I would miss you so much, but it would make me happy to know you were happy."

He had smiled gently, the indulgent smile an older brother gives his romantic younger sister. "If Gott had wanted me to live in Ohio, I would have been born in Ohio."

"That doesn't make any sense," she'd argued. "If someone so special to you lives there, maybe it's a sign from Gott that His plan involves you moving there."

"Family is everything," he had insisted. "I couldn't leave you and Daed behind. And I wouldn't ask you to come with me—Daed's business is secure here, he's happy enough…if not lonely." Their father had made a vow never to remarry following the passing of his wife.

"We would both understand if you left. That's all I'm trying to say," she'd insisted.

"Family comes first. You're my family. If Gott intends for Rachel and me to be together as a married couple, He'll make it so."

Levi's words rang in Leah's ears as she stood beside his casket. She could almost remember the way the fire had set his auburn hair aflame, the way he'd smiled when he assured her he'd rather stay in Lancaster to be with his family than move to Ohio to be with his special someone.

He always put family first, didn't he? He was utterly devoted to his father and sister, to the point where he'd put aside the love he felt for Rachel. Why would he then kill himself over her marriage? The question gave Leah a clearer sense of purpose than ever. She had to find out exactly how her brother had died, because she believed less than ever that he'd taken his own life.

"Are you sure this is a good idea?" Jonah asked. They sat in his buggy outside the furniture shop owned by Mr. Yoder. "I wonder if he'll want to talk to us."

"To me," Leah reminded him. "You'll be talking about furniture."

"I'm not sure what I'm supposed to say," he reminded her.

"Think of something fast," she said, checking to be sure her kapp was firmly fastened before climbing from the buggy. She heard Jonah let out a sigh of frustration as he followed her. She knew it wasn't much of a plan, showing up at the shop in hopes of catching Mr. Yoder in a talkative mood, but it was better than sitting around wondering how he was dealing with Levi's death. She'd heard he took it hard, but wanted to see for herself. He might be able to give some insight into Levi's state of mind that day.

The mood inside the shop was somber, tense. Leah felt it the moment she stepped over the threshold. It had been a week since Levi died. She wondered when things would ever get back to normal there.

Craning her neck to see into the back room, Leah noticed Amos working at sanding down a rocking chair. It was easy work—she could have done it herself. He wasn't working with any actual tools, the way the other craftsman were. It was a very telling scene.

Jonah cleared his throat loud enough to be heard. Amos looked up, then smiled when he recognized the pair by the door.

"Hello," he said, going out to greet them. "What brings you here today?"

Leah looked up at Jonah, giving him a pointed stare. He cleared his throat again. "My mamm needs a new rocking chair," he said, sounding unconvincing. It seemed to be enough for Amos, though, since his eyes lit up. Leah realized he was excited to make a sale, and felt sorry that the whole thing was a ruse.

She stepped away as though to leave the two of them to their discussion, eyeing up the back room through the open doorway. She saw a half dozen men employed in work, but no Mr. Yoder. His voice didn't ring out through the place, either—the man's loud, ringing voice was legendary in the community. He struck fear in the hearts of grown men. Levi had often made her laugh at stories of how even the biggest and strongest of the community often were reduced to silence in the presence of Mr. Yoder.

He wasn't there. Leah's heart sank, though she did her best to appear unaffected. She only looked around with the sort of curiosity a person would show while inside the shop their deceased brother had spent much of his time in. She wondered how many of the half-finished projects in the workshop had been started by him. She wished she could touch them, to feel a little of his presence. She wished she'd let him make a new rocking chair for her when he'd asked if she wanted one—she'd protested at the time, telling him there were more important things for him to spend time working on. How foolish she'd been.

"Leah, how are you?" Amos approached her with a sad smile.

"As well as can be expected, I suppose. And you?"

"Nothing's the same here, as you can see." He shrugged. "We do what we can."

"Yes, I'm sure you do. I notice your father isn't here. Is he well?"

Amos's eyes hardened. He wasn't the overly solicitous friend anymore. "He's well. He's taken Levi's death harder than any of us expected."

Leah felt sorry for Mr. Yoder, and wished she could speak with him. She kept her thoughts on him to herself, though, to avoid upsetting Amos. It was clear he didn't like his father's strong reaction to Levi's death. It was probably the guilt Amos felt, she reasoned, since he felt he shouldn't have let Levi wander off alone in that mental state.

"Can I ask you something? Something about Levi?" She whispered it, to avoid being overheard by any of the other employees.

"Of course," Amos replied. "What do you want to know?"

"What were his last words to you that day?"

Amos appeared puzzled, scratching his head. "Let me think. See, it's difficult. Had I known they would be his last words…"

Leah understood right away. "Of course. You would have paid attention. How silly of me. It's not as though you wrote them down." She felt foolish.

"It's not silly, Leah. Not at all. I'm sure I would want to know, too. I'll have to think about it some more. I know that once I stop thinking, it will come to me."

"That's usually the way it happens, isn't it?" She smiled. "What was his disposition?"

"Like I said before, he was quiet. Brooding. Troubled. I tried to find out what was troubling him so, but he kept to himself. It was useless, trying to get the information from him. I eventually gave up—not that I didn't want to know, but I knew it was no use. He became agitated with me, in fact."

"Agitated?" That wasn't like Levi at all.

"Yes, he became annoyed when I wouldn't stop asking questions.

That was when I decided it was best to leave him alone, rather than pressing the issue. I didn't want to start a fight." He laughed quietly, bitterly. "As though that mattered, considering what happened."

Leah noticed Jonah watching and listening quietly, as always. He didn't say anything, merely nodding his head from time to time. It was a comfort to have him with her, and to know she could discuss things with him later on. It was always better to have his point of view, since he was so thoughtful and looked at things from all angles.

"Where exactly did the two of you part ways? You said you were inquiring at the mill about lumber—was that it? I don't quite remember."

"Yes, it was at the mill," Amos agreed. "Well, not exactly at the mill. We hadn't reached it yet, but that was our destination. He sort of…wandered away while I stopped to talk with a few people."

"Which people?" Leah looked Jonah, excited at the notion of having more witnesses to question.

"Well, I really don't remember. Random passerby, people from the community. You know, talking about the weather. One of them—I think it was Mr. Lapp—said he felt rain coming on, since it bothered his arthritis so much. That I do remember, because it started raining not long after that."

"Yes, it rained much of the day and evening," Leah remembered, chewing her lip while thinking about the odds of old Mr. Lapp remembering anything from a week earlier. He was in his eighty-fifth year and not as sharp as he once was.

"You never noticed that he left you?" Jonah asked. "Was that normal for him?"

"Nothing he did that day was normal for him," Amos pointed out. "I wasn't sure what to do, honestly. I felt it best to let him think things out on his own. He was always the best worker here. It was hardly the first thought on my mind that he would shirk his duties. I said to myself, there has to be a very good reason for him to act this way. I knew my father would feel the same way were he there, so I didn't think to go after him—besides, I didn't think he would want me to. You didn't see him. You don't know the mood he was in." Amos shook his head, as though remembering that day. He looked at Leah and Jonah, and Leah saw the distress in his face. "Believe me, please. I ask myself every day, over and over, why I didn't pursue him. I hate myself for letting him walk off, alone. I hate that I was too busy doing business to go after my friend. I'll ask every day for Gott's forgiveness."

Leah took pity on him, as she did on his father. Both men were obviously very troubled in the aftermath of Levi's death. Amazing, she thought, how many lives we touch without knowing the depth of the influence we have on them. If she had told Levi the way his death would affect the community, he would have laughed and told her she was crazy. He never saw himself as anything special —that wasn't just his way, but the way of the Ordung. The Amish did not seek conscious fame or popularity.

"We'll leave you now," Jonah said, talking Leah by the elbow and holding it in a tight, no-nonsense grip. "We've kept you from your work for long enough."

"Yes, and there's so much to make up now that Levi isn't here." He sighed, then nodded to the two of them before returning to the workshop behind the showroom.

It wasn't until they were in the buggy that Jonah let out a sigh.

"What is it?" Leah asked.

"I don't know. Something about his story doesn't feel right. It seems as though he's hiding something."

"What do you think it could be?"

"I'm not sure. Something Levi said, maybe, or something he did. I feel like Amos is covering up for him. I can't shake the feeling. Don't you feel that something is off?"

"I do," Leah admitted, "but I didn't think you would take me seriously if I told you."

"Why wouldn't I take you seriously?" he asked. "I always take you seriously."

"But I know you want me to learn to accept what happened to Levi," she pointed out.

He only gave her a soft, caring smile. "But I take you seriously, though. I always do."

"All right," she agreed. "You always do."

Later that evening, she brought two glasses of iced tea out to the porch, where Jonah sat waiting for her. They'd stopped at the bakery on the way back from the furniture shop, and Mr. Kauffman was too busy to visit for long but did tell Leah he wouldn't be home in time for supper. Jonah had jumped at the opportunity to offer to keep company with her, Leah noticed. She'd gladly accepted—it wasn't easy being alone.

She sat beside him, handing a tall, cold glass to him before taking one for herself. It was nice to sit back and relax after a long day. Early evening was always her favorite time, after the supper dishes were finished and the kitchen cleaned. She could finally take time for herself to breathe, think, pray. Or sit on the porch and let the cool evening breeze remind her of Gott's presence all around her. He was everywhere, just as the breeze was.

"What are you thinking about?" Jonah asked. She turned to him, noticing—not for the first time—how very blue his eyes were. He had beautiful eyes, to go with his beautiful, wheat-colored hair and fair complexion. He was an extremely good-looking man, a fact that wasn't lost on many of the girls in the community. He had been a regular topic of whispers and giggles and every gathering since he reached his mid-teens and grew tall and strong.

It took Leah a moment to remember what she'd been thinking about before she looked into Jonah's eyes. "I…oh, yes…I was thinking about how much I love this time of day. More than any other time. It's the best time to think and pray and be. Just be. I love the peace, you know? That sort of tired but happy peace."

He nodded, sitting back in the rocking chair beside hers. "I sometimes think about getting older. Do you ever think about that?"

"Not overmuch," she admitted with a soft smile. "From time to time."

"I think about it. I think about having a home of my own, one day. With a farm like my daed's. And I imagine having a wife by my side, and children. I imagine going in after a long day's work and enjoying the time spent with my family. Sitting on the porch with my wife, talking about the day, watching the sun set." He took a sip of his drink, rocking slowly back and forth.

Leah was he looked away, or else he would've seen the deep blush which colored her cheeks. Didn't he hear what he was saying? Talking about sitting on the porch with his wife, when that was exactly what the two of them were doing together at that very moment! If he realized what he said, and its implication, he didn't show it. Either that or he had meant it, knowing full well how Leah would interpret it.

It wasn't as though she'd never thought about him in that way, though it was never of her own accord. It was the others in the community, assuming the two of them were already a couple, which planted the idea in her mind. She'd never suddenly looked at him and realized he was the man for her. She had only considered him, and whether or not she thought they would work together in that way. So far, she hadn't thought so. He was so different from her, more like a brother than anything else. She remembered the way Levi had fallen head over heels for Rachel the minute they met. That was what Leah was waiting for—the sudden spark of interest, the certainty that she'd met the person she was meant to be with.

"A lot of good that did Levi." She didn't realize she'd whispered it aloud until Jonah asked her to repeat herself. She blushed again, feeling silly for revealing her thoughts that way. She thought of some way to rephrase it, so it didn't sound as though she was thinking about romance with Jonah.

"I was thinking about what you said, about wanting to have a family one day. I know Levi wanted the same thing. He thought he'd found his chance when he met Rachel. A lot of good it did him."

Jonah nodded, reasonable as always. "I've been wondering about Rachel, now that you mention her." He stretched his long legs, clad in a pair of plain black pants, sighing.

"Wondering what about her?"

"How long did she know she was promised to this other man in

Ohio? Was it a traditional courtship? Writing to your brother with the news she would marry another man in a month…it seems very sudden."

"That's true," Leah conceded. "Especially if they'd been writing to each other for a long time. Wouldn't she have mentioned it?"

"She might have refused to believe it," Jonah theorized. "Or maybe she hoped Levi would come through for her, step up and claim her as his."

Leah giggled. "Levi would never do that," she said.

"Why not?"

"He wasn't the type. He felt things very deeply. I don't see him taking a train to Ohio to rescue the girl he loves from marriage with another man, is all. He's the type to hold his feelings inside, until…" She stopped short. Until he couldn't bear the pain any longer. Until he did something terrible.

Jonah stepped in before she could become too morose. "I'm thinking about Rachel's fiancé. What sort of man is he? The jealous type, maybe?"

Leah slowly began to understand what Jonah was getting at. "Do you think he might have done something?"

He shrugged, drinking his tea before answering. "I don't know. I don't know the man, I can't say what he would do. I only know that if he's the jealous type, he might have found Levi's letters to Rachel. If he and Rachel have been betrothed for a while, he might have become enraged at her writing to another man all this time. It's just an idea."

"It's a very good idea!" Leah assured him. "I hadn't thought of it. I knew I'd be glad we talked tonight."

"Oh, you did?" he asked, and she heard a teasing note in his voice. She grinned.

"Yes, I did. I'm usually glad after we talk."

"Why?"

She shrugged, looking for the right words. "I don't know, because you always help me see things with different eyes, I suppose. Whenever I lose my way, you help me back to where I belong. And you've been more help than I can describe this past week. I mean it. I can't thank you enough."

"You can try," he teased, but there was real warmth in his voice. "You don't have to thank me, though. Really. I don't do it to be thanked."

"Why do you, then?" She couldn't believe the question came from her mouth. What a brazen thing to ask! She didn't want to put him on the spot—he didn't deserve it.

He stayed silent, just rocking back and forth. He appeared to be ready to let the question sit without answering.

***

Jonah could hardly believe Leah was serious whenever she asked a question like that. Why did he do it? Why did she think? He'd only loved her for years. Quietly, from afar, but no less deeply.

What was it about Leah which drew him to her? Was it her sense of humor? The sweet earnestness in her eyes? Was it the way her temper sometimes got the better of her, making her cheeks glow pink and her eyes snap? She always looked beautiful when she got angry—sometimes he teased her just so he could see her that way.

Why hadn't he ever told her? He asked himself all the time why he couldn't get up the courage to admit his feelings. He wasn't that sort of person. He didn't have the courage to put their friendship in jeopardy—what if she didn't feel the same? It could ruin everything. Besides, it was a well-known fact that once a girl started thinking of a boy as a brother or "just a friend", that was it. She would never change her mind. He'd be a friend until the day he died, with no chance of her seeing him in any other light.

That would have to be enough. He knew it would be torture when she finally found the man with courage enough to tell her how he felt. It sent pain to his heart whenever he imagined her courting someone else. He wasn't strong enough to witness it for himself.

He could have his pick of any of the girls in the community. That was the funniest part of all. He knew they had crushes on him, and it wasn't as though he hadn't been interested in anybody else for his entire life. Once or twice a girl had caught his eye, made him wonder what it would be like to spend time with her. But he was never interested enough to go through with it. Levi used to laugh at him, teasing that he was too afraid to go with a girl. Jonah let him believe that, since there was no good way to tell him he was really in love with Leah. That was the sort of thing one friend didn't say about another friend's sister.

Of course, she was the woman he thought of when he imagined his life with a wife and family. It was becoming difficult to conceal his true feelings from her, but it needed to be done. All he could do was hope Leah saw him differently one day, and until then be the best friend he could be to her.

***

Leah wondered why her thoughts were going in that direction. It was strange, thinking of Jonah that way. Did he have feelings for her? Had she been wilfully blind all along? Maybe it was easier for her to think of him as a friend, a brother, a confidant. It was unfair to him, too, holding him at arm's length, relying on him for friendship and support while never giving him what he wanted from her. She couldn't keep him dancing on a string forever, like a toy.

There was no reason why she shouldn't like him that way, she knew. He was the most eligible young man she knew, and she already had a deep, true connection to him. They were already halfway to what could be a very fulfilling relationship. Did she dare take the chance of destroying them, though, if things went wrong?

He glanced at her, his forehead creasing as he read her expression. "What are you thinking about that has you looking so confused?"

She only shook her head, smiling a little. The fading light concealed her blush, which was a relief. What would he think if he knew she'd been wondering what it would be like to kiss him?

There was no forgetting what Jonah had talked about the night before, on the porch, when he brought up Rachel and her fiancé. Exactly what had Levi been writing to Rachel, and what had she written back? She was half-sure he would have burned or thrown away the letters—Levi had never exactly been sentimental, as so many men weren't—but there was a chance they were somewhere in the house. She needed to find them if they were.

She was alone, her father having gone off to the bakery many hours earlier. Once her chores were finished, she slipped upstairs. It was the first time she'd go into Levi's room since the night he disappeared, when she found their daed asleep on Levi's bed. They'd never discussed it, of course. She hadn't wanted him to know she saw him there.

Opening the door was like opening the memories of her heart, and within moments, Leah was overcome with emotion. It was exactly as he'd left it when he went to work that day. He'd stopped at home for his midday meal, and she'd handed him the letter from Rachel before heading out to do the week's shopping. She'd been at the farmer's market when Jonah found her to tell her the bad news.

When her brother had left the house that afternoon, it was as though he had every intention of returning. That was one thing which struck her as odd. If he'd intended to kill himself, wouldn't he have left some sort of clue? Something to ease the pain for her and their father? Nothing in his bedroom gave her any indication that he hadn't intended to return home later in the afternoon.

What a terrible thing, to go through the belongings of a loved one. She ran her hands over his plain, dark-colored shirts, hanging on their pegs. They smelled like him, she realized, and she held one of them to her nose. The tears flowed hard and heavy. Oh, Levi. Why did you do it?

He didn't do it. She couldn't make herself believe it, and nothing anybody else said would convince her. She reminded herself of the purpose of going through the bedroom, and forced herself to get back on track.

Beneath the bed were a few boxes. One of them held little trinkets he'd carved over the years—Leah was thrilled to find them, and wept as she ran her fingers over the intricately carved animals and people. They were the projects he would work on when he had leisure time, usually while the two of them sat by the hearth on cold nights. She'd always wondered what he did with them when he was finished. He'd kept them all that time. What a treasure.

The second box surprised her. It held a kapp, a pair of reading glasses and a thimble. Leah instantly recognized them as having belonged to their mother. He'd never told her he kept them. There were so many secrets hidden in her brother's heart—when she'd thought she knew him so well. Perhaps there was more to him than met the eye. Perhaps it wasn't unthinkable that someone as sentimental as he would commit suicide after having his heart broken.

The third box held letters, dozens of them. Leah felt as though she were invading his privacy by flipping through them, but she needed to know more about Rachel's intended. Had she ever mentioned him? Or did she toy with Levi, only telling him at the last minute? She was sure word would have Gotten to Rachel's community by that time. How did the other girl feel, knowing her one-time sweetheart was gone? Leah took a deep breath, reminding herself it wasn't Rachel's fault.

They had loved each other—it was clear. Rachel's letters were so full of hope, of wishes that would never come true. She wished her father would accept the idea of her marrying Levi, instead of insisting she marry someone with a large land holding. She wished she had the courage to run away to Lancaster, to marry Levi in secret and build a life with him. She wished she were a stronger person, one who had what it took to make her dreams come true. Levi was her only dream, her only hope. Leah cried again when she reflected on the beauty and longing in Rachel's letters. Poor Rachel. After reading everything, Leah considered writing to her, hoping to provide a little comfort.

So it wasn't as though Rachel made a secret of her father's misgivings. She was open about the way he actively sought a "better" husband for his daughter. Maybe he really had sprung this mystery man on her at the last minute. Who was he? Would he make the trek to Lancaster to have it out with his soon-to-be-wife's true love?

It was late in the afternoon by the time Leah finished reading. She put the letters back in the box, placing it gently beneath the bed. She only kept the figurines for herself, and was just about to put them in her room when a pounding knock at the front door jarred her, making her gasp. The house had been silent up to that moment.

She hurried downstairs, wondering what the trouble could be. No one knocked that way unless something was wrong. She peered out the window beside the door to find Amos standing there, hands in pockets, rocking back and forth on the balls of his feet. He looked anxious, on edge. Leah opened the door.

"Amos! What brings you here. Do you want to come inside?" She motioned for him to step in, standing back to give him room.

He only shook his head, his eyes wild. "I've got to show you something. It's extremely important. I found it just off the bridge… you know, the one where I saw Levi."

Leah's eyes widened. "What? You went back there? Amos!"

"I had to," he insisted. "I couldn't live with myself. I had to go back there, to see what he saw, to feel what he felt. I've been losing sleep over it, I really have. But I'm glad I went, because I found something important. You have to come and see before it's gone —I can't believe it's still there after a week."

"What is it?" Leah only had time to ensure her kapp was properly fastened and to grab a sweater from the hook before she ran onto the porch and down the steps, following close behind Amos.

"You'll see when we get there. I can't describe it," he said. She had to nearly full-out run to keep up with him. He was tall, with a long stride, and he was already nearly trotting to get to the bridge as quickly as possible. Along the way, Leah noticed dark clouds rolling in from the west. A storm was coming, and a big one. It made her think of the storm the day Levi died, and she shook her head to clear the thought. It was no time to indulge in such thoughts, not when she was on the verge of finding something important in her brother's death. She was glad Amos had spent more time thinking things over, even if it had caused him sleepless nights. If it meant finding out the truth, it was worthwhile.

Roughly a half mile from the bridge, the rain began to fall. Leah pulled her sweater closed, still running behind Amos. She ducked her head to avoid being blinded by the heavy downpour which seemed to fall from the sky in sheets. Rain ran down the back of her neck, making her shiver. She hadn't thought to bring a coat or an umbrella, having left the house in such a hurry.

"Come on!" Amos called, getting further away from her. She could hardly see, and once they reached the grassy banks of the river the footing was dangerous slippery.

"Amos!" she cried, trying to reach him while slipping in the mud. "We should go back! It's dangerous!" As if to confirm her words, thunder rumbled in the distance. Lightning would be close behind. It was rare to have a thunderstorm during the cooler months, but not unheard of. "Amos, we might get struck by lightning, or swept away. Let's come back later!"

It was as though he couldn't hear her. She wanted to turn around and run home—she could make it in ten minutes, maybe less—but she didn't want to leave him alone, either. If he fell or slipped, he would need help. Alone, he might be swept off with the river's current. It was already moving swiftly past, the heavy rain causing it to swell over its banks.

"Amos!" She screamed it, straining to be heard over the downpour. It was like she imagined cannon fire to sound. She looked around, noticing how they were the only two people around. If he were hurt, nobody would ever know. She wanted to leave, but couldn't. It was as though he were obsessed with showing her what he had found. "Amos, please! We have to go back!"

She finally reached him. He stared off into the river, standing on the bank with his fists in his pockets. It seemed as though he were lost in thought—probably blaming himself again for letting Levi go off on his own, Leah thought. She placed a tentative hand on his shoulder. "Amos? We should go. We can come back later. It isn't safe."

He turned his head so swiftly, water shot off the brim of his hat in all directions. His eyes blazed. It was enough to make her take one step back, then another. The fire in his eyes.

"What—what's wrong, Amos? What's happening?"

He sneered at her, and in an instant everything became clear. He didn't have anything to show her. He had only lured her there.

She backed away, her feet sliding on the wet grass. "Amos? What's wrong? Come on. We should go." She spun around, intending to run as fast as she could in the opposite direction, but he was too fast for her. He sprang, his arms closing around her like a vice. She screamed her head off, kicking her feet, trying to punch him. It was like punching granite.

"What are you doing?" Leah screamed, trying to fight him off. It was no use. He was too strong.

"Don't you know by now? You're so smart, right? Always asking questions, coming around the shop, wanting to know if I remembered anything. Asking after my father. As though I care what he does—as though he means anything to me anymore."

"I don't understand," Leah insisted. "What does this have to do with me?"

"Everything. You got too close, is all. If you had only behaved like a woman should behave and minded your own business, none of this would be happening. Just like if your brother had left my father alone and been a son to his own father, nothing would have happened to him."

Leah's blood ran cold, and her heart nearly stopped. It all came together.

"You?" she asked, the word coming out as a sob. "It was you?"

"Very good," he said, his mouth against her ear. She shuddered at the contact. "You finally figured it out. I knew you would. Which is why we're here, right now."

"I wouldn't have figured it out, Amos! You didn't have to do any of this," she insisted. "Really."

"Well, it's too late now," he chuckled. "I've already told you." He released her, though he blocked the way. She couldn't run around him without backing up first, and that would mean stepping closer to the bank of the river. The water came closer with every minute as the rain continued to fall.

"I don't understand why you did this," she said, hoping to stall long enough for someone to come by. But who, in that weather?

"You don't? You mean your perfect brother never came home with tales of how perfect he was? How my father put him on a pedestal, while he treated me like nothing? For years, I had to put up with that. Always falling short of the perfect Levi. The son my father wishes he had. You know he hasn't come out of his room for more than a few minutes at a time all week? He's been in mourning. Mourning!" Amos laughed, throwing his head back. There was no happiness in his laughter, though.

"He would never act that way if I died," Amos said, his voice bitter. "He wouldn't care at all. Business as usual, I'm sure. If anything, he'd be glad to not deal with me anymore. I hold up his work. He can't trust me to do a good job without constant supervision. He doesn't know that the constant supervision is what makes my life so hard! I can't succeed at anything with him breathing down my neck, waiting for me to mess up!"

He laughed again, this time quietly. "He would never treat Levi that way. Oh, no. He stood back and smiled proudly whenever Levi finished a project. He would even compare me to Levi right in front of me, and he'd shake his head and ask me why I couldn't be more like him. Can you imagine that?"

She shook her head. "No, I can't. It's terribly unfair to you. Everybody thinks so."

"Oh, they do?" Amos sneered.

"Yes. We all know he's too hard on you, Amos. I've always thought it was a shame." Leah's eyes cut left and right while she searched desperately for a way out of there. It seemed there was nothing she could do but keep him talking. Maybe if he talked long enough, he would wear himself out. It was the only chance she had.

"I've seen the way you look at me," he said, advancing on her.

That wasn't the way she wanted things to go. She took a step back, then another.

"What do you mean, the way I look at you? How do I look at you?"

"Like you know something. Like you don't believe me. The stupid police believed me. Why couldn't you? Why wasn't it enough that your precious, perfect brother saw how miserable his life was without his silly girlfriend, and so he jumped off the bridge? What was so unbelievable about that?" When Leah didn't answer, Amos did it for her. "Because he was so wonderful. He wasn't cowardly, right? He wouldn't throw away Gott's gift. He would turn toward Gott, instead. Am I right? He would draw closer to his family and you would all pray for him to find a way out of his sadness. I'm right, aren't I?"

Leah could only nod. That was pretty close to what would have happened. She and her father would have supported Levi no matter what. Amos nodded in return, smirking.

"Right. Perfect Levi and his perfect family. You should have left well enough alone, Leah."

"How did you do it?" she asked. "I need to know. How?"

"The same way I brought you here," he said. "I told him what he needed to hear. In his case, that it looked like someone was struggling in the flood waters further downriver. It had rained a lot in the days leading up to then. Do you remember? So the river was already moving fast and hard. He stood on the bank, trying to see what I told him I saw. I didn't see anything, of course, but the hero had to try to save someone—even if it meant harm to himself. When he wasn't looking, I picked up a rock and smashed him over the head with it."

Leah covered her mouth with her hands, a long cry escaping her lips. Oh, poor Levi. He had never seen it coming, had never Gotten the chance to defend himself against the pitiful coward who'd killed him.

"I filled his pockets with rocks," Amos continued, "then I threw him off the bridge. I thought the force of him hitting the water would account for the wound to his head, and the flood water would make it harder to find the body. When the rain started again, it was like a stroke of good luck. For once, I felt like I did something right."

His eyes darkened. "Until you wouldn't let it go. It wasn't good enough for you. I knew he got that letter from Rachel, and I knew what it said. He thought we were friends, you see, and he told me about it as we walked. I knew it was the perfect excuse for him to kill himself. That was when I knew the time was right. Everybody would have believed it—and everybody did. Except for you."

He took another step, and this time Leah slipped and fell on her backside as she tried to escape. The ground was all mud at that point, saturated by the heavy rain. It still fell, blurring her vision, making it nearly impossible to see straight as she scrambled backward to avoid Amos's approach.

"Don't worry," he said. His words were soft, soothing, almost like a lullaby. "I'll make it fast, the way I did for your brother. See, I'm merciful. More merciful than he ever was to me. I wouldn't make him suffer for years the way he made me suffer. He never knew what hit him. I'll make it that way for you, too. I promise. And just think, you'll be with him again soon. Doesn't that make you happy?"

Leah half-screamed, half-sobbed as the reality of Amos's words hit home. He was going to kill her, and she'd made it easy for him by walking straight into his trap. No—she'd run into it. She closed her eyes, saying a quick prayer to Gott to take care of her father. And of Jonah. Sweet Jonah, who she knew in that moment she loved more than anyone in the world. She hoped he felt it in what she knew was her last moment on Earth.

She opened her eyes, ready for Amos to do what he intended to do. There was nowhere for her to go.

Suddenly, a savage cry from over her shoulder. Amos looked up, eyes wide with surprise, then a blur of action as another man leaped at him, knocking him to the ground. The man's hat fell off, and Leah saw the golden blond hair beneath. It was Jonah.

Leah got to her feet, backing away from the scene as the two men wrestled for their lives. They were so dangerously close to the water's edge—all Amos would have to do would be to buck Jonah off from on top of him, throwing him into the river.

"Jonah! Watch out! You're close to the water!" He must have heard her, for he dragged Amos further away from the bank's edge by the collar of his jacket. Then he hauled him to his feet. Leah thought it was all over—Amos was no match for Jonah, who was much stronger and better developed from his work on the farm.

She was wrong, however. Amos was crazy enough to drive his head into Jonah's midsection, making him gasp as he fell backward onto the ground. Leah screamed as Amos landed a solid blow to Jonah's face. Jonah held Amos's wrists, pushing them away from his face. Leah realized with horror that Amos intended to strangle Jonah, and in the force of his fury just might be successful.

"No!" she screamed, running over to where the two of them fought. She pulled Amos by the hair with both hands, yanking him backward. He howled, swinging back in her direction, but she jumped deftly out of the way while Jonah used the element of surprise to his advantage. He jerked his right hip up in a sharp, sudden movement which caught Amos off-guard and sent him flying. Jonah rolled with him, pinning the smaller man to the ground.

He must have known he was beaten, for he fell silent after that. Just in time, too, since the police arrived moments later. How they knew where to go, Leah didn't know. She only knew she'd never been more relieved to see anyone in her life.

That wasn't totally true, she realized, as Jonah stood to allow the officers to pull Amos from the ground. Jonah was the sweetest sight she'd ever seen. His eye was blackening and his clothes were a muddy mess, but he was beautiful to her.

She went to him, and he held his arms out. "In case I never get the chance to tell you this again," she said, "I love you." She had been sure she'd never get the chance to tell him. It was funny, how out of everything she might have regretted, holding herself back from what had been there all along had been the biggest regret of all.

He didn't say anything for a long time. It was enough for them to hold one another while the police took care of Amos.

Hours later, they sat together in the kitchen at the house. Leah's father was there, holding his daughter's hand.

"I can't believe I almost lost you both to him," he murmured, squeezing her hand so hard it hurt. She wouldn't have asked him to ease up for anything in the world, though, knowing how important it was for him to remind himself that she was there, out of danger, safe at home.

"You didn't, though. Thanks to Jonah." She beamed at her savior, who sat with a handful of ice against his black eye.

"How did you know where to find her?" Mr. Kauffman asked.

"I got here around the time the storm started," Jonah explained. "Mr. Stoltzfus was just coming from the other direction when I reached the main road after finding Leah wasn't home. He told he he'd seen her and Amos running off toward the river. I knew there was something wrong, so I headed there myself. I got there just in time." His voice was tight—it was clear he remembered the scene as he found it, with Amos standing over Leah.

"Gott put you there at the right time," Leah's father said. "It's the only explanation."

"Me and Mr. Stoltzfus," Jonah smiled.

"And you're sure he didn't hurt you?" Mr. Kauffman turned to Leah, his eyes searching hers. "You're sure?"

"He didn't," she assured him for what must have been the fifth time. "I promise. He would have, if Jonah hadn't appeared when he did. He thought I was too close to finding out the truth about Levi."

"And you would have, given the time," Jonah pointed out.

"Maybe, maybe not. It never would have occurred to me that Amos was truly capable of something like that." She shivered, remembering the hatred in his eyes and voice when he talked about her brother. "He did a good job of hiding his true feelings from the world, for sure."

"He wouldn't have been able to hide them forever," Mr. Kauffman pointed out wisely. "There was a lot of talk around the community.

It wasn't only you who doubted Levi would take his own life. It was all I ever heard whispered in the bakery. How unthinkable it was, how there had to be some other person involved. The only problem was, no one could imagine who would hurt him."

"Maybe Mr. Yoder could," Leah mused. "Maybe that was why he locked himself in his room—not just because Levi died, but because he knew Levi would never kill himself. Because he knew he'd sent him out with Amos that afternoon. He might have worked it out on his own." It was unimaginable, the guilt he must have carried in his heart if that were the case. It would explain him shutting himself off from everything, even his business.

"How terrible," Jonah murmured. "I'm sure it couldn't have been easy for Amos—not that I'm defending him, of course. I only wonder how much a person can take before they lose leave of their senses. Amos clearly lost his."

"Yes, clearly." Neither of them would ever know how truly depraved he'd sounded when he told her all about killing her brother. It had sounded like he enjoyed recounting the story, like he revelled in his final victory over his enemy. And Levi had never suspected a thing.

The rest of the evening passed in much that manner, with Mr. Kauffman finally agreeing to go to bed and let his daughter out of his sight by the time the clock struck ten. Leah was tired, too— one the rush of panic had worn off, her body had ached and felt more fatigued than she could ever remember feeling. Not just from where she'd fallen, but everywhere. A good night's sleep would be just what she needed.

First, there was a matter of business to attend to. Jonah stood, taking his hat from the peg by the door, then turned to her. "Can I ask you something?"

"Of course. Anything you want."

"Did you mean it?"

Leah's heart swelled with emotion, and it gave her the courage to say what needed to be said. "When I thought Amos was going to kill me—when I was certain I had breathed my last breath—there was only one thing I could think to be sorry for. I had never admitted to myself that I loved you all this time. I had never told you. And if you don't feel the same way, that's all right. I understand. I just couldn't go another minute without you knowing, is all."

Jonah appeared to mull this over with his characteristic thoughtfulness before he smiled. "If I don't feel the same way? Do you think I make it a habit to save women every day?" He held his arms out to her as he had by the river, and she rested her head on his shoulder as she had then. It felt right.

"Did you hear?"

Leah looked up from the display case at the bakery. She'd been spending a lot of time there in recent months, knowing how important it was to her father that she be nearby. It had been over half a year since the incident with Amos, yet he still fretted over her. She indulged him, knowing that once she was safe for long enough, he would relax again.

"Did I hear what?" she asked Mrs. Miller, who had just run in from outside.

"Amos Yoder has been sentenced to forty years in prison—at least."

It was a sobering thought, Amos spending most of his life in prison. He would be an old man by the time he got out. The judge had not been lenient, as so many had speculated he might, seeing as how the case involved Amish people. Many gossips in the community were certain he would take pity for some reason. They had clearly been wrong.

"I'm sure you feel relief, knowing he'll be safely behind bars," Mrs. Miller continued.

"Relief? Not really," Leah admitted. "He needs help. I hope he gets it there." She knew there were doctors who could treat him. Maybe he would get out in time to still make something of his life. Maybe he still had time to find the happiness she had found.

She excused herself, going into the back room to share the news with her father before anyone else did. He paled a bit when he heard, then nodded resolutely. "It's as it should be," he said. "I'm sorry for his father. We've both lost a son."

Yes, but you loved your son, Leah thought. It was a rare occurrence, Mr. Yoder showing his face around town. He was virtually a recluse. Leah still wasn't sure if it was embarrassment over what Amos had done, grief over losing him, or a sense of guilt. Amos had made certain his lawyers, and thus everybody in the community, knew that he blamed Levi and his father for what he had done. Mr. Yoder seemed to age more than a decade overnight, his shoulders suddenly slumped, his hair whiter than before.

"How do you feel about it?" Leah's father asked.

She thought it over. "I'm not sure. It won't bring Levi back," she pointed out.

"No, it won't."

"I'm grateful to Gott that the truth has come out, though. Even if it meant getting myself into trouble."

"You didn't just get yourself into trouble," her father reminded her. "You nearly lost your life." It was the same argument they'd had innumerable times over months since Amos's arrest.

"But I didn't," Leah reminded him, as she always did. She kissed his cheek before going back out to the front of the bakery. It would be a relief when he loosened his grip a bit.

By the time the bakery closed for the night, Leah was sore from head to toe. It had been a particularly busy day, and she knew why. Everybody wanted to see how she felt, to ask questions without really coming out and asking what they wanted to know: was she glad Amos had received the highest sentence possible?

She wasn't glad, and she told anybody who would listen. Just because he'd caused her family pain and taken her brother away didn't mean she wished him undue harm. The very idea went against everything she'd been taught from her earliest days. Gott's law didn't change just because her heart had been broken.

Jonah was waiting for her in his buggy when she locked up. Mr. Kauffman had already gone home for the evening—she'd forced him to, since his health was still questionable after the blow he'd suffered. He was looking better, though, and eating better as well. It would just be a matter of time before things returned to anything near their old "normal".

"You don't need to pick me up, you know," Lean grinned, even as Jonah helped her into the buggy.

"Are you joking? Your father would have my hide if I let you walk home alone." He grinned before starting out for the Kauffman house.

"Does he really make you do this?" she asked, growing serious.

"He doesn't make me do anything. I'm just glad to have an excuse to be over-protective." Jonah winked at her, and she scowled in response. It looked as though she'd spend the rest of her life with them watching her like hawks.

She didn't mind, as long as Jonah was the one doing the watching…and as long as it was really for the rest of her life.

As though he could read her thoughts, Jonah cleared his throat. "Actually, your father and I just finished a meeting at your house."

"A meeting?" She waited for explanation.

"Yes, you see…we discussed the possibility of our marriage. Yours and mine, I mean. Not mine and his." He chuckled nervously at his own joke. Leah was unable to speak. She could only stare blankly at him.

"You're not making me feel very confident," Jonah murmured, glancing at her as he drove up the dirt path to her front door. She shook herself, breaking free of her shocked silence.

"What was the final decision?" she asked, her voice quiet.

"He told me it was up to you, but he was all for it."

Leah nodded. "Then it seems there's nothing else to decide." She beamed, unable to keep up her serious act any longer.

"You will, then?" he asked, his voice cracking with nervous tension.

"Of course, I will." They laughed together, both of them overflowing with joy. If there was one small grain of happiness Leah could take from the nightmare of losing her brother, it was the reminder that love shouldn't be horded and wasted. It had to be expressed and shared for it to do any good. She made a vow in Levi's memory to never forget that important lesson as she gazed lovingly into the eyes of her best friend and future husband.

I would like to thank you for taking the time to read my book. I really hope that you enjoyed it as much as I enjoyed writing it.

I have been writing Amish books for Amazon for almost two years now, almost exclusively on Kindle. However, due to growing demand I managed to get the majority of my titles available in paperback versions. There is a list of all of my kindle books below, bit by bit they are ALL going to be released in paperback so please keep checking them.

If you feel able I would love for you to give the book a short review on Amazon.

If you want to keep up to date with all of my latest releases then please like my Facebook Page, simply search for Hannah Schrock author.

Many thanks once again, all my love.

Hannah.

LATEST BOOKS

DON'T MISS HANNAH'S BRAND NEW *MAMMOTH AMISH MEGA BOOK* - 20 Stories in one box set.

Mammoth Amish Romance Mega Book 20 books in one set

Outstanding value for 20 books

OTHER BOX SETS

Amish Romance Mega book (contains many of Hannah's older titles)

Amish Love and Romance Collection

MOST RECENT SINGLE TITLES

The Orphan's Amish Teacher

The Mysterious Amish Suicide

The Pregnant Amish Quilt Maker

The Amish Caregiver

The Amish Detective: The King Family Arsonist

The Amish Gift

Becoming Amish

The Amish Foundling Girl

The Heartbroken Amish Girl

The Missing Amish Girl

Amish Joy

The Amish Detective

Amish Double

The Burnt Amish Girl

AMISH ROMANCE SERIES

AMISH HEARTACHE

AMISH REFLECTIONS: AMISH ANTHOLOGY COLLECTION

MORE AMISH REFLECTIONS : ANOTHER AMISH ANTHOLOGY COLLECTION

THE AMISH WIDOW AND THE PREACHER'S SON

AN AMISH CHRISTMAS WITH THE BONTRAGER SISTERS

A BIG BEAUTIFUL AMISH COURTSHIP

AMISH YOUNG SPRING LOVE BOX SET

AMISH PARABLES SERIES BOX SET

AMISH HEART SHORT STORY COLLECTION

AMISH HOLDUP

AN AMISH TRILOGY BOX SET

AMISH ANGUISH

SHORT AMISH ROMANCE STORIES

AMISH BONTRAGER SISTERS 2 - THE COMPLETE SECOND SEASON

AMISH BONTRAGER SISTERS - THE COMPLETE FIRST SEASON

THE AMISH BROTHER'S BATTLE

AMISH OUTSIDER

AMISH FORGIVENESS AND FRIENDSHIP

THE AMISH OUTSIDER'S LIE

AMISH VANITY

AMISH NORTH

AMISH YOUNG SPRING LOVE SHORT STORIES SERIES

THE AMISH BISHOP'S DAUGHTER

AN AMISH ARRANGEMENT

AMISH REJECTION

AMISH BETRAYAL

THE AMISH BONTRAGER SISTERS SHORT STORIES SERIES

AMISH RETURN

AMISH BONTRAGER SISTERS COMPLETE COLLECTION

AMISH APOLOGY

AMISH UNITY

AMISH DOUBT

AMISH FAMILY

THE ENGLISCHER'S GIFT

AMISH SECRET

AMISH PAIN

THE AMISH PARABLES SERIES

THE AMISH BUILDER

THE AMISH PRODIGAL SON

AMISH PERSISTENCE

THE AMISH GOOD SAMARITAN

Also Out Now:

<u>The Pregnant Amish Quilt Maker</u>

Eve King is a very independent and headstrong young Amish woman. Until she met Jeremiah that was. Theirs was a love written in the stars and she quickly came to depend upon him in all areas of her life.

But when Jeremiah is tragically killed in a horrible accident she finds herself alone and afraid. She holds a secret close to her heart. A secret she's been ignoring for too long. A secret that may ruin any chances she might have at ever being truly happy again.

Then Gabriel Esh finds a way into her life. He is clearly smitten with the beautiful young widow. However, she realizes that she can't seem to ever see a time when she could love him back the same way.

Will he be able to accept only part of her heart? Will she even give him the chance? Just like the quilts she so beautifully pieces together, will Eve ever be able to piece the broken shards of her heart back together? Will the secret that Eve holds stop any chance the pair have for a future together. Will Gott's mercy prevail and bring the two young people together?

Here is a Taster:

Clearfield County, Pennsylvania, Early March…

Eve looked up from the quilting frame as the bell over the door to the small quilt shop tinkled, letting her know a new customer had just entered the store. She watched as two Englisch women slowly wandered around the shop, gently fingering the quilts displayed on wooden hangars.

"Oh, I just love the colors in this one," the younger of the two women remarked. "I could never sew like this."

"This is one of the best reasons to visit here," the other woman remarked. She looked up, spying Eve sitting in the opposing corner and smiled at her.

"Good morning. Are these your quilts?"

Eve stuck her needle in the fabric to she wouldn't lose her place and stood up, smoothing the black apron down as she walked around the wooden frame, "Some of them. Many women in the Amish communities around here display and sell their quilts in this shop."

"Well, I have to tell you I'm so jealous of your talent. Do you happen to know who made the purple and blue wedding ring quilt there?" The younger woman pointed back to the quilt that had first captured her attention.

Eve smiled at her, "That is one of mine. It is a wedding ring pattern."

"Yes, and the colors are so vibrant." The woman shared a smile with her, "My sister is getting married at the end of the month and I wanted to get her and my future brother-in-law something extra special. I think that quilt would make a wonderful wedding gift."

Eve inclined her head, "I will fit a king sized bed."

"Perfect! I'll take it."

"Wunderbaar!" Eve wrote up the ticket and was pleased to see that the women had indeed come prepared with cash. So many of the Englisch came to the small shops expecting to use their credit cards or write checks. While some of the shops that were owned by the Englisch accepted credit cards, the Amish-owned stores did not.

She carefully removed the quilt from the hanger and lovingly folded it, before placing it inside the brown paper sack. "Denke," she told the women as they happily received their purchase and left the shop.

Eve rubbed her temples, hoping the Jeremiah was already on his way to pick her up. She had married Jeremiah King the previous November, and even now she was amazed at how she'd changed.

Eve had met Jeremiah when he had come to her parents' quilt shop, where she worked, to repair a leaky roof. Her daed had recently injured his knee and when Jeremiah had stopped by to offer his assistance, he'd gladly accepted the help.

Eve had been twenty-two at the time, and Jeremiah had been twenty-four, just recently celebrating his birthday a few weeks earlier. He was a cabinetmaker and carpenter in his daed's shop and when he and Eve had first met, it had been a case of love at first sight.

The ever independent and headstrong young quilt maker had tried to ignore her attraction to him, but Jeremiah had kept at it, and six months after their first meeting, they had become engaged. Jeremiah had won not only her heart over, but her head as well.

Eve had gladly learned to relinquish control to him, something she knew had made her parents very happy. For far too many years, Eve had insisted on doing things herself, to the point of defect. The other young menner of their Ordnung had found it hard to deal with Eve because she always had an opinion and didn't mind sharing it. An odd trait for most Amish.

Jeremiah, rather than being offended and turned off from pursuing a relationship with her, had seen her independence as a challenge. One he'd gladly met and conquered. She smiled as she thought back to how diligent he'd been in his pursuit of her affections.

Jeremiah was very handsome and she thanked Gott daily for blessing her with such a gut mann. She walked around the small shop, straightening up here and there and then quickly sweeping the wooden floorboards. Before getting married, she would have closed the shop when she wanted and driven herself home, or walked the three miles without complaint.

But Jeremiah was very careful with his fraa and insisted on driving her to and from work. He also had insisted on her keeping standard hours at the quilt shop. Eve had listened to his request and his reasoning and gladly complied. Another change from her normal behavior patterns prior to meeting the love of her life.

Jeremiah had become her world, secondly only to Gott and on days like today, she had trouble remembering what life had been like before meeting him. She was just putting the broom away when the bell over the door announced another visitor.

She stepped out, prepared to announce that the shop was closed, to see Jeremiah standing inside the shop rubbing his hands together briskly. She smiled warmly at him and loved the feeling of her heart speeding up. She was so in love with her husband and she grinned as she remembered they were going to have an indoor picnic today to celebrate the day they had first met.

It had been Jeremiah's idea and one she'd wholeheartedly agreed with. It was much too cold to have a picnic outdoors just yet, but that wouldn't stop them from pretending and enjoying being with one another. Jeremiah had built them a lovely home and she was looking forward to putting in a garden, come springtime, and helping her husband pick out the farm animals they would add at that time.

"Ready to go?" Jeremiah asked, leaning forward and kissing her cheek. Public displays of affection were frowned upon in their community, but Jeremiah never ceased to greet her in the same way. It had drawn more than one smirk and raised brow from the elders in their Ordnung, but Eve found she didn't really mind. She loved knowing that Jeremiah cared for her and had missed her while they were apart.

"Jah. It was a gut day, I sold another quilt."
"That's great news. One of your own?"

"Jah. An Englischer bought it as a wedding present for her sister. Are we still having our picnic?" she asked, thinking ahead to the things she still needed to do to complete their evening meal.

"We are and I have another surprise for you," he told her as she locked the quilt shop door. He led her to his buggy and handed her up, pulling the thick lap blanket from behind the seat and tucking it around her legs.

Eve watched him jog around the horse, climbing into the buggy a moment later. "What kind of surprise?"

Jeremiah winked at her, "I stopped by the diner and had Mary Anne put together a picnic dinner for us. You, my lovely bride, do not have to cook tonight."

Eve leaned over and kissed him on the cheek, "Denke. That is a very nice surprise."

Jeremiah reached for her hand, and started them on their journey home. Eve sat back and enjoyed just being with her husband. One day they would have a familye to take care of, and she was following a piece of advice given to her by her mamm on her wedding day. Enjoy the time you have with your husband alone, for once the children start arriving, finding time alone with one another will take much work.

Eve was doing her best to heed that advice. And she'd never been happier.

Middle of May, an hour after dark…

Eve glanced towards the front door once again, listening carefully to the storm that raged outside. When she didn't hear anything but the howling wind and rain hitting the window panes, she bent her head back to the quilt she was piecing together.

She tried not to let herself worry that Jeremiah hadn't come home yet. He'd picked her up from work, as usual, and then told her he needed to visit a shop on the edge of town and check some cabinet measurements. He'd promised to be home in a few hours, and she'd laughingly promised to have his dinner ready and waiting for him.

She'd decided to wait to eat with him, and currently the casserole she'd made was sitting on top of the stove keeping warm. The rain had started up a little while after Jeremiah had left, and when a loud crack of thunder shook the haus, she put her quilt pieces down and walked to the large window.

She could see the drive and the storm as it moved around her. This was the first summer storm they'd had, and almost three weeks earlier than normal. She briefly wondered how her corn was holding up, it was barely a foot off the ground, and even a strong wind was liable to bend the stocks over. But as much as she wondered, she wasn't inclined to step out in the storm to check it out.

As one hour passed into the next, Eve began to grow worried. Jeremiah was always punctual and it was so unlike him to be gone for this long, she grew anxious. The storm had abated somewhat, but still Jeremiah did not come home.

When she could stand the worrying no longer, she pulled a quilt around her shoulders, grabbed the lantern sitting by the front door, and headed towards the her parents' haus. It was mile walk through the fields, and she was muddy and soaked through by the time she stood shivering on their front doorstep.

She knocked on the door loudly, hating the fact that she was waking them from their slumber, but knowing there was something wrong. Her daed answered the door, took one look at her, and hollered for her mamm to join him.

After telling him about Jeremiah's errand and failure to come home, her daed hitched the horse up to the buggy and headed towards the emergency phone some two miles away. Her mamm took her into the kitchen and heated water for tea, offering her a towel to dry herself with.

Eve spent forty-five minutes trying to concentrate on the mundane topics her mamm used to try and keep her from worrying, and by the time her daed returned, she was a nervous wreck. He entered the house, a look on his face she'd never seen before.

"Dochder...," he paused at a loss for words. Her mamm seemed to understand what he wasn't saying and she started crying. Eve looked at her and then back to her daed, "What's wrong?"

"Eve, there was an accident. The state police are on their way here...," the sound of car doors slamming stopped his speech. "That will be the police now." He turned and Eve had a horrible feeling in the pit of her stomach. "Daed?" she called after him, dread filling her heart as her mamm continued to cry softly.

"Eve, these are the men from the State police. They need to speak with you about Jeremiah." Her daed made that statement very stiffly, holding back his emotions.

Eve looked to the men, moving her gaze back and forth between theirs. They looked very sorrowful and she whispered, "You know where Jeremiah is?"

One of the officers stepped forward, "Mrs. King, it is with great sorrow that I must inform you...your husband was involved in an buggy accident this evening."

Eve felt her heart stop and she clasped her hands at her throat, "Where is he? Is he hurt?"

"Mrs. King, one of the wheels on the buggy misaligned and caused the buggy to overturn."

Eve nodded as such accidents were known to happen from time to time. Usually the occupants of the buggy suffered only minor scrapes and bruises, occasionally a broken bone. "Thank you for coming to tell me. Was he in need of medical attention?" That was the only reason she could come up with for why Jeremiah had not allowed them to bring him home.

"Mrs. King, your husband's injuries from the buggy accident were only minor, but his buggy overturned at the junction between the highway and the road leading into town. With the storm and the rain…a large delivery truck wasn't able to brake in time to avoid hitting him."

Eve gasped and she saw her daed and mamm reach for her as she crumpled to the floor. "Where…Jeremiah…," she sobbed, unable to speak for the sorrow that was breaking her heart in two.

"Ma'am, I'm sorry, but her didn't make it. Your husband is dead."

Your husband is dead. The words replayed in her head as the sound of her anguished cry filled the small kitchen. She vaguely heard her daed thank the officers and make arrangements for the body to be brought back to the local undertaker.

Her mamm tried to console her, but Eve felt like a part of her had died. They had both been so happy. Gott, why?

Her mamm helped her upstairs to her old room, helping her remove her apron and muddy shoes. Her mamm helped her change into a borrowed nightgown, poured some water onto a cloth and wiped her face for her, but the tears just kept coming.

Eve knew she needed to get control of herself, but she couldn't come up with a reason to do so. Her mamm sat by her bedside throughout the night, and Eve cried herself to sleep over and over again.

When the first beams of the sun peeked through the window, her eyes were puffy from crying, her body ached, and her stomach was protesting even the slightest movements. Her head ached from crying so hard and for so long.

"Eve, you need to get up and wash your face. I'll bring you some clothes to put on. Come downstairs to breakfast and we'll see what needs to be done." Her mamm's words were soft, and she could feel the love behind them, but Eve simply wanted to stay in bed and let the world go on without her. How am I supposed to do anything without Jeremiah by my side?

She put on the clothing her mamm brought her, but she made no other effort to make herself look presentable. She refused to eat anything, and when the elder council arrived to go over the details of Jeremiah's funeral, she simply got up from the table and walked out the back door.

She walked home without really remembering doing so. Her daed had called her back, even sending her bruder after her, but she ignored them both. She arrived home half an hour later, told her bruder to go home, and locked herself inside.

She headed for the bedroom, but the thought of lying in the bed she'd shared with Jeremiah was much too painful. She pulled the quilt from the bed, hugging it to her and savoring the lingering smell of her husband.

She curled up on the couch, crying herself into a fitful sleep on and off throughout the day. Sometime in the afternoon, she woke up and drank a glass of water and ate a piece of the bread she'd made the day before.

Several people came to her front door, but she ignored them all. When the sun set and the rooms grew dark, she lit a single